CHRIS BELL
COURTNEY HOPKINSON

Australia • Brazil • Japan • Korea • Mexico • Singapore • Spain • United Kingdom • United States

Trapped

Fast Forward
Purple Level 19

Text: Chris Bell
Illustrations: Courtney Hopkinson
Editor: Cameron Macintosh
Designer: James Lowe
Series designer: James Lowe
Production controller: Seona Galbally
Audio recordings: Juliet Hill, Picture Start
Spoken by: Matthew King and Abbe Holmes
Reprint: Jennifer Foo

ISBN 978 0 17 012649 6
ISBN 978 0 17 012645 8 (set)

Cengage Learning Australia
Level 7, 80 Dorcas Street
South Melbourne, Victoria Australia 3205
Phone: 1300 790 853

Cengage Learning New Zealand
Unit 4B Rosedale Office Park
331 Rosedale Road, Albany, North Shore NZ 0632
Phone: 0508 635 766

For learning solutions, visit cengage.com.au

Printed in Australia by Ligare Pty Ltd
7 8 9 10 11 12 13 20 19 18 17 16

Evaluated in independent research by staff from the Department of Language, Literacy and Arts Education at the University of Melbourne.

TRAPPED

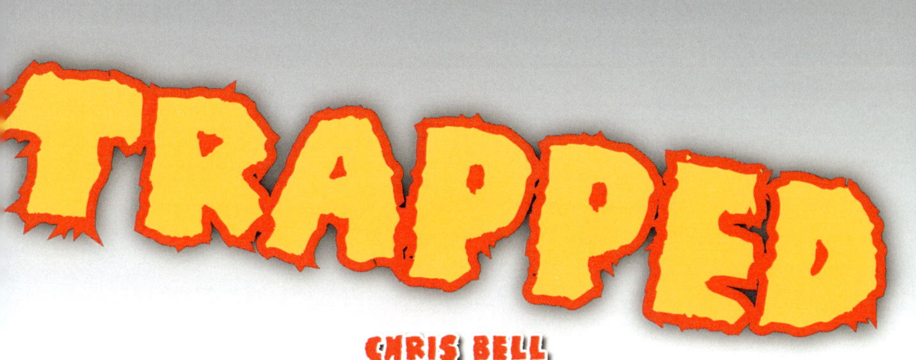

CHRIS BELL
COURTNEY HOPKINSON

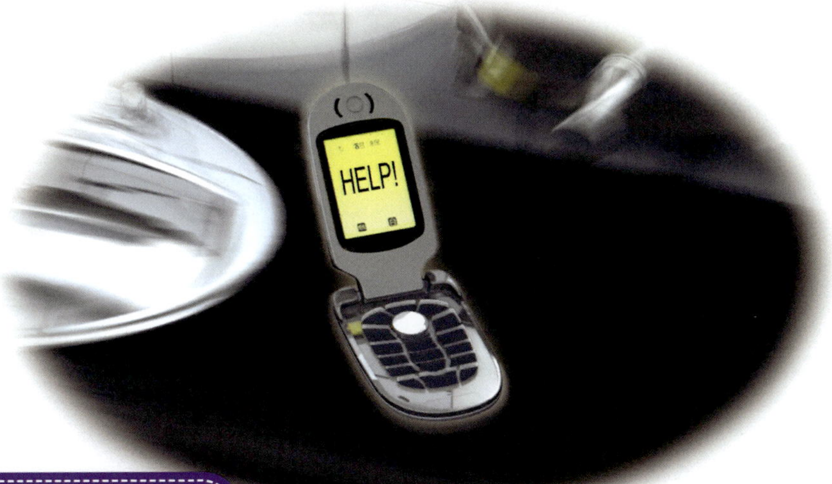

Contents

Survival

"Are you listening, Tom?"
asked Mrs Wyatt.

Tom's eyes snapped open wide.
He nodded to his teacher.

Mrs Wyatt stared at him, then said,
"Now, who knows how to signal
a passing ship for help
with a mirror?"

Tom sighed.
Why did he have to learn
about survival?
It wasn't likely he'd ever be stranded
on a deserted island.

Sure, the SOS beat was catchy –
three short taps, three long taps,
then three short taps again.
But if I were really stranded,
Tom thought,
I'd just use my mobile phone.

Tom jabbed Khoa beside him and whispered,
"Not many deserted islands around here!"

Khoa smiled and nodded.

The class clock ticked slowly. Tom felt his eyes start to grow heavy again.

Trapped!

"Bye!" shouted Tom,
after basketball practice.

Khoa waved and disappeared
out the school gate.
The rest of the team had already
been picked up.
Tom checked the time on his phone –
it was nearly six o'clock.
Home was only a couple of minutes
walk away,
but he really needed to go
to the bathroom.

The school was almost deserted.
Even Harvey, the cleaner,
had packed up by now.

Running Words 189

BANG!

A loud noise echoed
from somewhere outside the bathroom.

"What was that?" asked Tom.

Then Tom heard a clang
as a wire gate slammed shut
and a lock was bolted.
Tom raced out of the cubicle …
Oh no!
The wooden outer door
was shut tight.
Tom tugged on the handle.
Nothing moved.
He yanked harder.
"Harvey. Open the door.
I'm locked in here!" yelled Tom.

Not a sound came back.
For a second, Tom couldn't believe it.
He was trapped.

Chapter 3

No Ship to Signal

A long time passed
and still no one heard Tom.
His fists ached from banging
on the door.
His throat hurt from yelling for help.
But no one came.

Then he remembered – the phone!
He snatched his mobile out of his pack.
Then he saw the blank screen.
Oh no ...
The battery couldn't be flat already!

Tom looked up to see his worried face in the mirror.
He almost laughed.
Here he was,
trapped with a giant mirror.
Only one problem – there weren't many passing ships around to see a signal!

Tom sagged down the wall
onto the cold floor.
He knew everyone would be worried
that he hadn't come home.
They'd come looking for him,
wouldn't they?

Chapter 4

Bathroom Blues

Tom tugged the zip on his pack shut again.
He didn't know why he kept looking.
There was still nothing to eat inside.

He stood up and stretched his legs.
Why didn't someone come?
Didn't anyone miss him yet?

A row of windows ran along the top wall behind the cubicles. Tom gulped when he saw how dark it was getting outside.

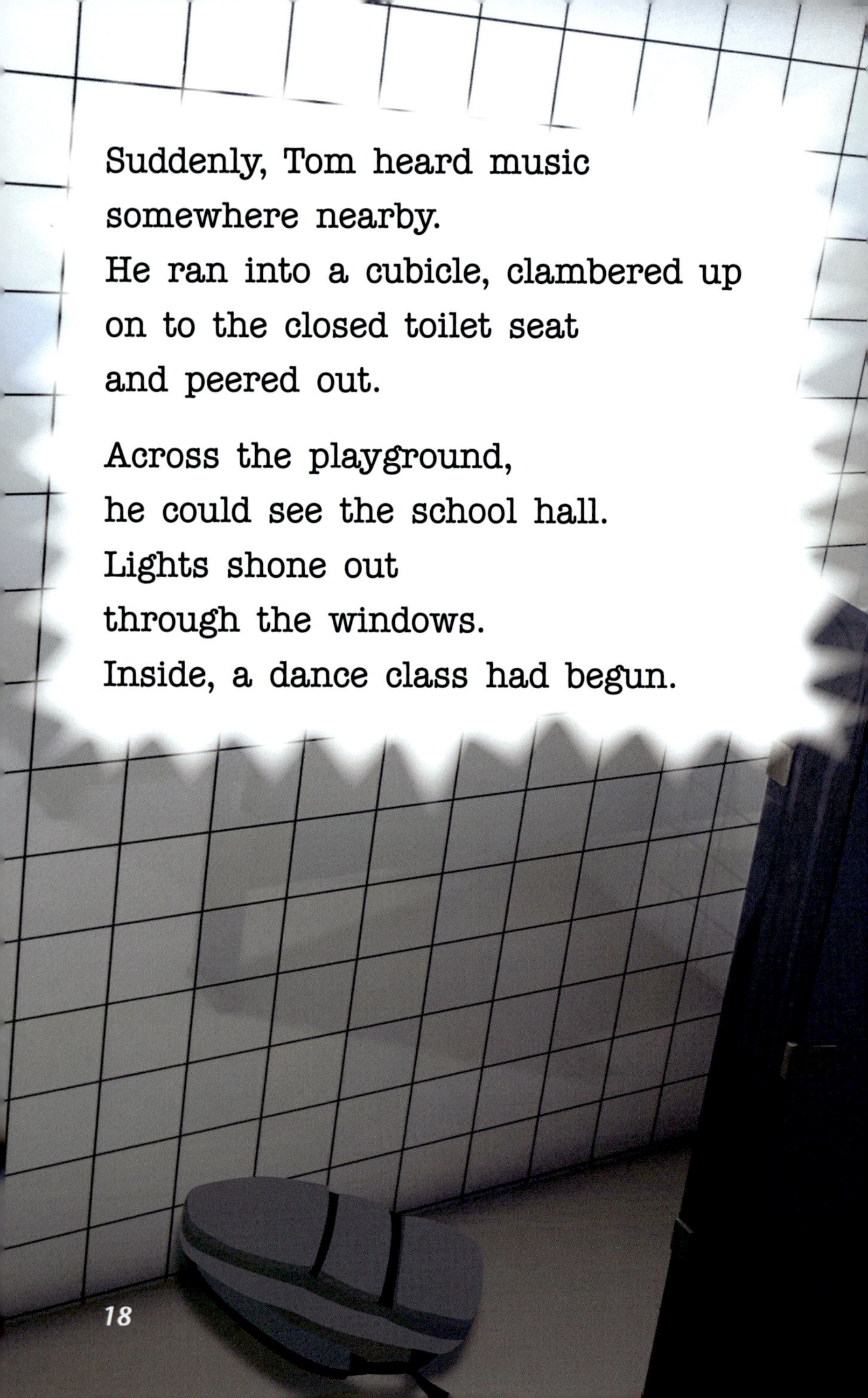

Suddenly, Tom heard music
somewhere nearby.
He ran into a cubicle, clambered up
on to the closed toilet seat
and peered out.

Across the playground,
he could see the school hall.
Lights shone out
through the windows.
Inside, a dance class had begun.

Tom banged hard on the glass,
but the music was too loud.
No one could hear him.
He'd have to wait until
the class finished.

Finally, the music stopped.

BANG! BANG! BANG!

Tom smashed his fists hard
against the glass.
Over in the hall,
no one even looked up.

BANG! BANG! BANG!

Still no one heard.

Great, thought Tom.
I know how to flash a passing ship
with a mirror.
I know how to send an SOS.
But I can't get rescued
from the school bathroom.
Unless ... No!
That'd never work ... would it?

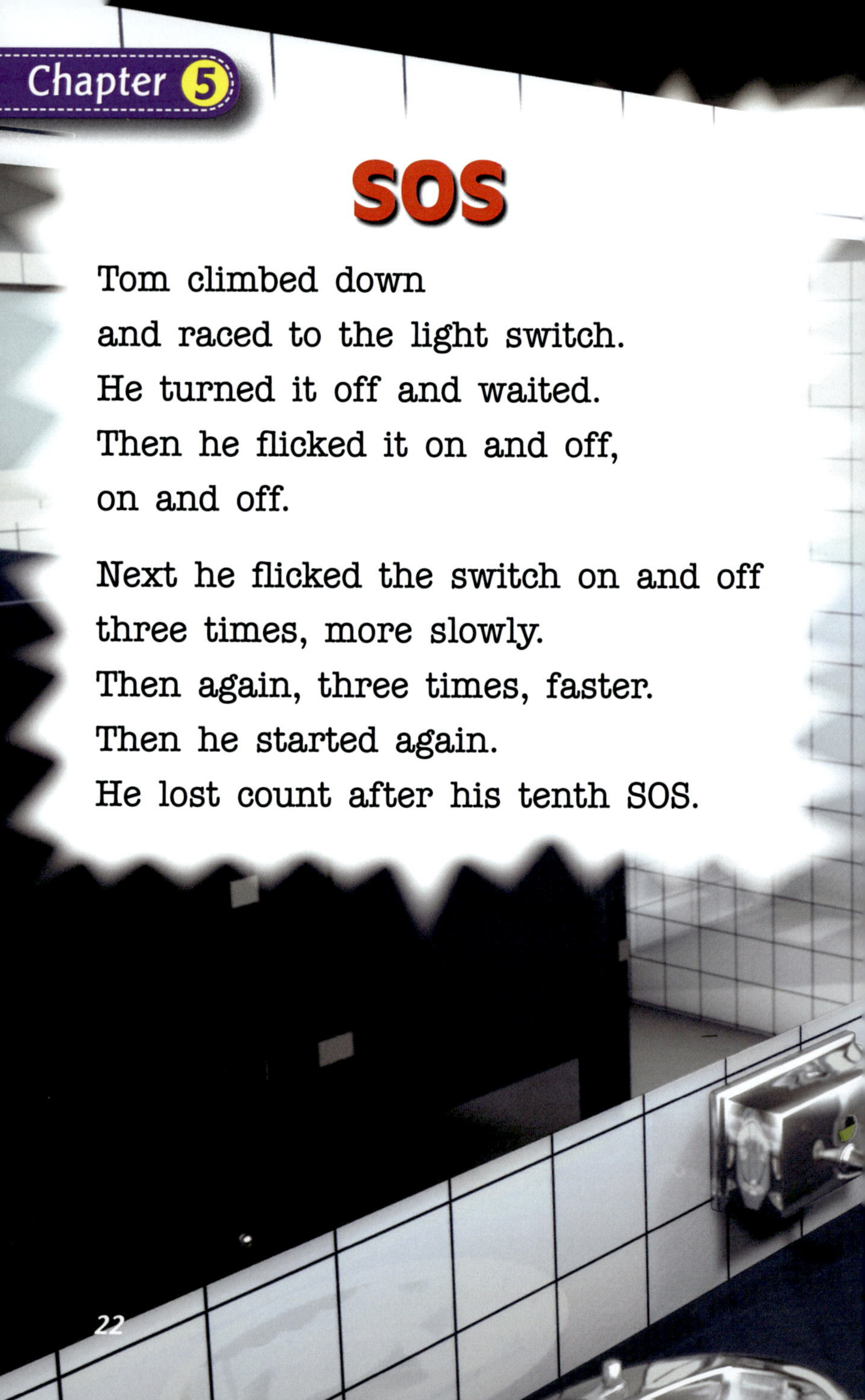

Chapter 5

SOS

Tom climbed down
and raced to the light switch.
He turned it off and waited.
Then he flicked it on and off,
on and off.

Next he flicked the switch on and off
three times, more slowly.
Then again, three times, faster.
Then he started again.
He lost count after his tenth SOS.

Suddenly ... what was that noise?
Was that the wire gate
slamming open?
Yes! Tom could hear footsteps
running towards the door.
"I'm in here," he yelled.

A key turned in the lock,
and the door flew open.

Harvey smiled at Tom.
"Just as well we saw your SOS.
You could have been trapped in here
all night,
instead of just a couple of hours."

Tom shook his head –
a couple of hours?
It felt like all night!

But Tom smiled back at Harvey.
At least he wasn't trapped any more.